John Wilson

Memorial Discourse on the Death of the Reverend Stephen Hislop of Nagpur

John Wilson

Memorial Discourse on the Death of the Reverend Stephen Hislop of Nagpur

ISBN/EAN: 9783337816575

Printed in Europe, USA, Canada, Australia, Japan

Cover: Foto ©Raphael Reischuk / pixelio.de

More available books at **www.hansebooks.com**

MEMORIAL DISCOURSE

ON THE DEATH OF

THE REV. STEPHEN HISLOP OF NAGPUR.

BY JOHN WILSON, D.D., F.R.S.

BOMBAY:

DEPOSITORY OF THE BOMBAY TRACT AND BOOK SOCIETY.
PRINTED AT THE "EXCHANGE PRESS," FORT.

1864.

PREFACE.

THE publication of the following discourse has been requested by many members of the congregation in Bombay to which it was originally addressed ; and by many Christian friends elsewhere residing who continue to feel that the missionary cause has suffered a great loss by the death of the esteemed, laborious, honoured, and devoted STEPHEN HISLOP, by whose sudden removal from this sublunary scene its delivery was occasioned. The author much regrets that, owing to unavoidable circumstances, its appearance should have been delayed to the present time. In printing the discourse, it has been thought right to expand it by enlarging the quotations originally made in it from Mr. Hislop's correspondence and other sources ; and to add to it, in an Appendix, a brief Note on the Results of his Geological Researches, and a very interesting account of his Last Hours, most kindly and considerately addressed to Mr. Hislop's bereaved and deeply-afflicted partner by R. Temple, Esq., Chief Commissioner of the Central Provinces of India. The pamphlet, as it stands, is inscribed, as an imperfect (and it is to be hoped only provisional) Memorial of the departed, to his numerous friends in India and in Britain, who remember and admire his work of faith, and labour of love, and patience of hope in our Lord Jesus Christ in the sight of God and our Father ; and this, with the earnest request that they may unite in the prayer, that the great Lord of the Harvest may speedily send forth many duly qualified labourers to the great field of our Eastern Empire, to take the places of those who have lately fallen, and to enter into important and claimant spheres of exertion and enterprize which have not yet been occupied.

Bombay, June, 1864.

DISCOURSE.

" He (Christ) gave some, apostles; and some, prophets; and some, evangelists; and some, pastors and teachers."—Ephes iv. 11.

THE term *apostle* is generally applied to those disciples of the Lord Jesus who were chosen and commissioned by himself to go and teach all nations—to do the primary work of instructing the peoples of the earth to whom they found access in the great facts of his incarnation, atonement, and exaltation. It was required of the twelve who formed their complement, on the first organization of the Christian church, that they should be of his followers who had accompanied him during his personal ministry, "beginning from the baptism of John unto that same day that he was taken up." They were special witnesses of the resurrection of Jesus, having themselves seen him and conferred with him, and participated in his gracious and potent influences, after his rising from the dead. When Saul of Tarsus was afterwards added to their number, he had this qualification, as well as those who had been appointed before him. Of this transcendently interesting man, on the personal appearance of the Lord to him near Damascus, the Lord said, "I am Jesus whom thou persecutest. But rise and stand upon thy feet : for I have appeared unto thee for this purpose, to make thee a minister and a witness, both of these things which thou hast seen, and of those things in which I shall appear unto thee." Paul, in consequence of the call and authorization which he thus received from the Lord, the peculiar revelations which were vouchsafed to him, the abundant labours which he was strengthened to perform, the remarkable sufferings and trials which he endured, and the unsurpassed success which attended his ministrations, declared himself to be "not a whit behind the chief of the apostles." He distinguished between himself as an apostle of Jesus, and the faithful men who laboured with him in the Gospel. Even when he allowed others to unite with himself in his epistles to the churches, he wrote with a distinct recognition of his own peculiar position:—" Paul, called to be an *apostle of Jesus Christ*, through the will of God, and Sosthenes *our brother*, unto the church of God which is at Corinth ;" "Paul, an *apostle of Jesus Christ* by the will of God, and Timothy *our brother*, unto the church of God which is at Corinth;" "Paul, an *apostle* (not of men, neither by man, but by Jesus Christ, and God the Father, who raised him from the dead ;) and all the *brethren* which are with me, to the churches in Galatia," and so in other instances. We are safe in holding, then, that though the term *apostle* ('ἀπόστολος) simply means one sent, it is restricted in the New Testament to the limited number of persons who were commissioned and commanded by the Lord Jesus, in his own person, to go forth to the work of discipling all nations. Others have been, and now are, the messengers of the churches, and sent forth according to the spiritual and providential call of Jesus ; but they are not apostles in the New Testament primary sense of the term.

The *prophets* mentioned in our text, like the apostles, are those of New Testament times ; for, with the apostles, they are introduced to notice in our context in connexion with the ascension of Jesus. Their designation was given to them, as can easily be shown, not because they necessarily or exclusively spoke of future events, but because they spoke, like the prophets of old, under the guidance of the Holy Ghost.

Of *evangelists* (literally, announcers of the glad tidings) mentioned in our text, as well as of apostles and prophets, it is said in the Form of Church Government agreed upon by the Assembly of Divines at Westminster, that they were extraordinary officers of the church which have " ceased." For this expression of opinion no scriptural authority is adduced. It probably originated in the belief that the evangelists were ministers of Jesus engaged in the work of evangelization exclusively under the immediate direction of the apostles. It may well be called in question, as it actually is by many devout and intelligent Christians. The designation " evangelist" occurs in the New Testament only in two other places besides our text.* In the first of these instances it is applied to Philip, who was also one of the seven deacons; and in the second, to Timothy, who is charged by Paul to " do the work of an evangelist." Philip, both at Samaria and on the road to Gaza, when he communed with and baptized the Ethiopian eunuch, acted independently of his fellow-labourers, and to a certain extent on the direct admonition of the Holy Ghost. Timothy, who did some ministerial service under Paul, did not cease to be an evangelist on the death of that apostle (if he actually survived him) or when at any time he acted merely under a sense of his own responsibility to God. An evangelist I consider to have been, in the scriptural sense of the denomination, a pro-

* Acts xxi. 8; 11. Tim iv. 5.

claimer of the glad news of salvation, without his being fixed to any particular congregation, and who engaged in carrying on the evangelistic work more especially among the unconverted. The designation is emphatically applicable to our modern missionaries, foreign and domestic, who bring glad tidings of good things to those who know them not. The work of these ministers of Christ is primarily and essentially that of evangelists. It was principally because the Church of Christ was for long very imperfectly discharging its own functions that the opinion was hazarded that their office had ceased.

Pastors and *teachers* are universally allowed to be continuous officers and agents of the Christian church.

Of the apostles, prophets, evangelists, pastors, and teachers noticed in our text, it will be observed that, whether ordinary or extraordinary, they are all spoken of as the gift of Christ. " Unto every one of us is given grace according to the measure of the *gift* of Christ." Wherefore he saith, " when he ascended up on high he led captivity (that is, all captivating powers) captive, and *gave* (it is *received* in the sixty-eighth Psalm here quoted, the reception preceding the gifts, and being for the gifts) —gave *gifts* unto men ; ... and he *gave* some, apostles ; and some, prophets; and some, evangelists; and some, pastors and teachers." Similar doctrine is taught in other passages of the New Testament, as in the twelfth chapter of the Epistle to the Romans, and the twelfth chapter of the first Epistle to the Corinthians. The inference from the whole teaching of the New Testament on the subject is, that the true messengers and ministers of the church are indebted to the risen and exalted Saviour for their qualifications for, and call to, their " work of faith, and labour of love, and patience of hope." It is no ground of exception to the statement that the majority of the apostles were designated to their office before the ascension of Jesus. It was only when they had received "power" after that the Holy Ghost was come upon them, that they were to be witnesses unto Jesus both in Jerusalem and in all Judea, and in Samaria, and unto the uttermost part of the earth. The baptism of the Spirit received by the Son, and sent by the Son on his ascension into heaven, was their real and effective ordination to their work. So it has been in reference to the true and devoted servants of the Lord, in agency and work, in all ages of the church. So it is at the present day. So it will be while saints require to be perfected, while the work of the ministry has to be done, while the body of Christ has to be edified. The only call to the office of the ministry approved by God is that which originates with God himself. It was the choice of God which the church at Jerusalem was anxious to ascertain in the selection of an apostle in the room of Judas (who was guide to them who took Jesus). Paul and Barnabas were called by God to the work of the ministry among the Gentiles, before they were set apart to it (by prayer and fasting) by the prophets and teachers of the Church at Antioch. It is Christ who, by his providence, raises up agents for his work, and who by his Spirit imparts to them that spiritual wisdom and knowledge which become available for the instruction both of his people, and of those who are ignorant and out of the way. It is He who gives that love to the person and cause of the Redeemer, that zeal for his honour and glory, that compassion for perishing sinners, that devotedness to the service of the Lord, and that faith in the power of his word, which constitute the essential qualifications for, and call to, ministerial office ; and all that man can do in the work of ordination is humbly to recognise these qualifications in those in whom they exist ; to bind over, by solemn engagements, those professing them to ministerial fidelity ; to commend them, by fervent prayer, to the divine blessing, in connexion with their work of faith, and labour of love ; and to grant them facilities for orderly and decent service in the bounds of the churches, or in the exterior parts of the world to which they may be sent. Divine grace is neither held nor bestowed by office ; and it is not office which secures grace, but grace which fits for office. It is the spirit of antichrist which teaches that man is the medium of calling down and dispensing, by tenure or functions of office, or by outward ceremonies and services, the grace of God needful to make either a Christian man or a Christian minister. The very act of prayer in ordination shows that ministerial grace is derived from that Holy Spirit whom the Saviour died to purchase, and lives to bestow.* Jesus himself continues to make and to give evangelists, pastors, and teachers. To Him, His Church must ever look for its workmen, in believing, fervent, and persevering prayer. Let faith in his power and willingness to provide agents for carrying on his own work be ever cherished and exercised. He who made one who was a persecutor, and a blasphemer, and an injurious instrument of evil, his disciple, minister, and apostle, will still do all that is needful to raise up messengers to convey his glorious gospel even to the ends of the earth.

The recognition of the ministers of Christ as his own gift is always becoming. There are times, however, when

---

* See Sermon by the author at the ordination of Mr. Hislop in " Evangelization of India."

this recognition of the evangelists, messengers, and ministers of the Divine Word as the gifts of the risen and exalted Saviour, is specially incumbent on the people of the Lord. One of these times certainly is when God, in his sovereign but all-wise providence, removes marked men among them from their work on earth to their reward and work in heaven. Our loss on these occasions is to be seriously estimated, and rightly improved. The examples set before us in providence, are to be considered and followed (as far as they are in accordance with the will of God) as well as those which are recorded in the Divine Word. When God speaks to us in a remarkable way by the sudden and unexpected, and impressive deaths of his servants, we have seriously to look to what is taken from us, as well as to the lessons which, in the solemn manner of his removing his servants, he is striving to impress on our souls.

Last Monday the following most affecting and grievous intelligence, with the substance of which you are all doubtless acquainted, reached us from our faithful and esteemed brother in the ministry, Mr. Cooper of Nágpur:—" With very profound grief, and deep solemnity of spirit at the mysterious providence of God, I have to communicate to you the unspeakably sad intelligence that my beloved friend and colleague, Mr. Hislop, is no more. He has been very suddenly taken from us, and in a way that we little anticipated. Early on Thursday morning the 3rd instant (September, 1863), he left Sitábaldí in good health and spirits to join the Chief Commissioner (of the Central Provinces of India), who had written for him to come and examine some tumuli at Tákulghát. This was done during the day of Friday; and in the evening while returning to Borí on horse-back, a distance of three miles, he fell into a deep *nalá* (tor-rent-bed) and was drowned. At the time of the melan-choly occurrence he was quite alone, and the night was very dark. The Chief Commissioner, Mr. Temple, had gone on before him, leaving two sowárs (horsemen) to escort Mr. Hislop to Borí, where dinner was prepared for the party. There is a Government school at Tákulghát ; and in order to have an opportunity of examining it, and delivering to the pupils his master's message, Mr. Hislop allowed darkness to overtake him, and then hurried to join the party at Borí. As the *nalá* had risen consider-ably, Mr. Temple found the place where they had crossed in the morning dangerous, and sent back a chaprásí (messenger) to meet Mr. Hislop, and tell him to cross a little further up. It seems that the chaprásí missed him in the darkness, and went on to Tákulghát seeking him. In the meanwhile our beloved brother had out-ridden the sowárs, and arriving at the very spot that was to be avoided, and probably not expecting any obstruction from the *nalá*, was suddenly precipitated into deep water ; and here, after a short struggle, the beloved father and founder of our Nágpur mission passed away into glory everlasting. The horse galloped on to Borí, and this was the first intimation to the friends there that something had happened. A search was then instituted, and after three hours the body was found in the water. Oh ! what a stunning blow it was to us all, and especially to his dear wife, on Saturday morn-ing, when the sorrowful news reached us. Captain Puckle, a Christian ¦brother, and one of the party, who but for sickness would have been with Mr. Hislop, when in all probability the melancholy event would not have occurred, wrote me the particulars. His letter was brought by a sowár, and Oh ! it is impossible to describe our feelings. Deep, very deep, and intense was our sorrow for the beloved partner who was expecting a joyful meeting with her husband that morning. With hearts like to break Mrs. Cooper and I went over to make known the sorrowful tidings to her. She met us with a smile that pierced us as a dagger; but from our countenances she soon surmised that all was not as usual. With wonderful composure and resignation she received the sad news, and ever since has been enabled to cast herself upon the Lord. As a mission we are plunged in deepest grief, and have a feeling of awful desolation. The words of the Psalmist best describe our state, ' I was dumb, I opened not my mouth, because Thou didst it'. ' Help Lord, for the godly man ceaseth ; for the faithful fail from among the children of men.' I can write no more at present. I know you will all pray for us, and especially for dear Mrs. Hislop. God only is our help and comfort."

How much lamentation and sorrow these sad tidings brought to us all in Bombay, and especially to us the brethren and fellow-labourers of the departed, it is unnecessary to say. Our sorrow is not merely for wife and children so sorely bereaved, though they (as the greatest sufferers in the case) are the objects of our deepest and most tender sympathy. It is also for ourselves, in whose small and feeble ranks in the warfare of the Lord in India, a faithful and devoted fellow-soldier and leader has fallen ; for the solitary mission in the central and remote part of the country, which has in a moment lost its zealous and able founder and father under Christ ; for the native and European churches at Nágpur, to whom with his colleagues, the departed so constantly, and prayerfully, and efficiently ministered ; for the Free Church of Scotland, whose first messenger, after its separation from the Scotch ecclesiastical establishment in 1843, he was to the heathen world, and whose band of labourers in India, notwithstanding great and peculiar encouragements, is still so limited ; and for evangelical Christians everywhere, sympathizing with the work of the Lord in this great but sin-bound land. All the parties here mentioned must feel this sore bereavement in no common degree, for it deeply affects the interests of them all. By some it may be spoken of as an " accident ;" but there are no " accidents" in the all-comprehending providence of God, which extends to every object which exists, and to every event which occurs. The hand of God was in actuality, though not in miraculous speciality, as really dealing with the pool of water in which our dear brother sank to rise to the regions of glory, as with the fiery chariot which Elijah entered to be conveyed to heaven. There were a great many circumstances concurrent in the case which are of a striking and impressive character, and which seem to indicate to us the purpose of God as to the actual issue. They are such as the delay in starting from the school by the way where Mr. Hislop terminated his zealous missionary labours ; his outriding his escort to get speedily to the resting-place of his honoured friend Mr. Temple ; the sudden rise of the river which he had easily passed in the morning ; and his missing in the dark the messenger who had been purposely sent to warn him of the danger which existed. But independently of these combined incidents, we have the assurance that in this, as well as in all other cases of the removal of the Lord's people from this sublunary scene, it is the determination of God which is carried into effect. Our bereavement is from the Lord; and it has been ordered in the exercise of that wisdom which cannot err, of that faithfulness which cannot fail, and of that love which is never wanting in the chastisements administered by our Heavenly Father. It is our duty to seek to know and to practise the lessons and duties which it emphatically teaches. Christ's gift of our brother to the evangelistic work in India, let us earnestly, though briefly, contemplate,—as well as the more prominent lessons to be learned from the withdrawal of that gift.

Mr. Hislop was born at Dunse, in Berwickshire, on the 8th September, 1817. He was trained up in the ways of the Lord by godly, affectionate, and prudent parents; and through the grace and mercy of God he became, it is believed, decidedly pious in the morn of life. He received his early education first at a private school, and afterwards at the parochial and grammar school of his native place—the same seminary, I would remark, at which a great hero of the liberties of the Christian Church, the late Dr. William Cunningham, Principal of the New College, Edinburgh (the most effective propounder and defender of the doctrines of the Reformation of modern times) received his primary classical education. He was preceded and encouraged in his studies by an elder brother, (one of my own intimate friends and fellow-students,) who is now a minister of the Free Church of Scotland, at Arbroath, and the author of an able and original work on the Papal Apostasy;* and by another who was for some time the Head of the Free Church Normal School at Glasgow, and who is now the proprietor of a very successful boarding school for youth seeking a liberal education. His collegiate

* The Two Babylons.

education he principally received at the University of Edinburgh,* where he was a distinguished student, honoured by his professors, and respected and esteemed by his associates, as a young man of genuine moral principle and piety, of amiable character, and of most promising talents and attainments. At the Divinity Hall of the same University, too, which, under the promptings and leadings of the word and Spirit of God, he attended as an aspirant for the Christian ministry, he enjoyed the lectures and tuition of the marvellously-endowed, devoted, and eloquent Chalmers; of the acute, and learned, and accomplished Welsh; and of the zealous, kind, and courteous Brunton, whose able services in the early years of our Indian missions we cannot forget. The last year of his theological studies was in the New College of the Free Church, under the two first mentioned professors and one of their distinguished surviving colleagues. He was chosen by Dr. Welsh to assist him in carrying his excellent work on Church History (of which he lived to publish only the first volume) through the press; and by his patience, learning, and research, he contributed a good deal to the verification and accuracy of its numerous quotations and references. With the study of the word of God he combined, what is so genial with it, the study of the works of God, of which the Psalmist says, "The works of the Lord are great, sought out of all them that take pleasure in them; his work is honourable and glorious...he hath made his work to be remembered." He looked to the depths below as well as to the heights above, and to the wide face of the earth on which he trod. To Geology, that late but fascinating science, he devoted his particular attention. In his native county he had

---

* He attended the University of Glasgow for one Session.

before his view the remarkable field of observation which so effectively excited and sustained the inquiries of a Hutton (James), a Playfair, and a Hall, who, notwithstanding some errors of theory, were among the fathers of British geology ; and in the vicinity of Edinburgh he had what has been appropriately called the natural Museum of the Science. He gave decided indications of pre-eminence in this department,though he was determined to pursue it only in subordination to the still higher wisdom —that of seeking to win souls to Christ. With his preparation in study for the ministry, he combined, in the families of Sir Alexander Wallace and Mr. Murray of Mouswald, at various times, the tuition of the young, which seems almost a necessary preparation for distinguished practical acquisition and appreciation of distinct knowledge, and for the successful communication of it to those of riper years.

There were several rather remarkable circumstances connected with the call of Mr. Hislop to the great work of an Indian Missionary. In 1842, my agency was asked by a most benevolent and able (and afterwards distinguished) officer of the Indian army (Captain, now Major-General, W. Hill, C. B.) towards the establishment of a Christian Mission, to which he was most willing to contribute for him the large sum of twenty-five thousand rupees, in the important but neglected field of Central India, with Nágpur as its head-quarters. I immediately addressed the friends of our missions at home respecting it (supported on the occasion by the concurrent judgment of the missionaries in India, including that of Dr. Duff of Calcutta, most cordially and vigorously expressed); but the growing and thickening troubles of the Church of Scotland prevented its receiving that attention which it merited. When I got to Scotland in the following year, after my long journey through the Lands of the Bible, I at once applied myself to the matter in view. There were difficulties in the way. The Free Church had to provide for its own wants, in the sustentation of its ministers, who, to preserve the liberties and independence of the Church, had in the noblest spirit surrendered the endowments which they had enjoyed from the State, according to the constitution of the country, invaded for the first time by a majority of the members of the civil courts; in the necessity of providing churches, manses, schools, and schoolmasters' houses, for the congregations and seminaries adhering to its communion, and thrown on its care; in the theological colleges which it had to form and support for the instruction and training of its candidates for the holy ministry; and in the provision which it had to make for the maintenance of the missionaries of the undivided establishment, who, whether labouring among Gentiles or Jews, had, without a single exception, adhered to its communion, and for their efficient encouragement in the different branches of their evangelistic enterprize. To talk of a new mission, and that in a new and difficult field in a native Indian State, in these circumstances appeared to some to be hopeless of the desired result; but it was made in faith, and as far as the resolution of the Foreign Mission Committee was concerned, it met with success within less than two months after my arrival on the shores of Britain. This was very much owing, under God, to the interpretation of the call from India which (not without his usual caution) was made by the hallowed and honoured Dr. Gordon, the Convener of the mission Committee, who, after the various explanations which he received, saw it to be clearly the duty of the

Church to follow, in regard to the case the "leadings of Divine Providence." I shall not despair of the abiding Christian liberality of a church which acted in this generous and blessed, because generous, way, in the circumstances now hinted at, whatever retrogressions in the support of Christian missions, from inattention or partial indifference, may, as at present, for a season occur.

The first concern of the parties thus interested in the matter was to look out for a suitable missionary. Where was he to be got in the multitude of newly-formed congregations needing pastors, and of stations needing preachers? Had he not been raised up, prepared, and given by the Lord himself,—by the risen and exalted Saviour who has received gifts for men, and who has the Holy Spirit and his influences at his disposal, he would not have have been found. The deep and genuine, but unostentatious, piety of Mr. Hislop, who was then concluding his extended course of study; his superior talents, and attainments in literature, science, and theology; his marked good sense, meekness of disposition, and soundness of judgment; his zeal and perseverance in the acquisition of diversified knowledge; his interest in the Students' Missionary Associations of the University and the New College; his kind attentions and courtesies to the beloved native convert, Mr. Dhanjibháí, who had accompanied me in all my journeyings to the West, and who had joined some of the classes which he was attending; his faithful and zealous discharge of the duties of the Secretaryship of the Female Society of the Free Church of Scotland for promoting the Christian Education of the Females of India, to which he had been called; and his manifest aspirations after usefulness in various ways, pointed him out as a desirable agent for mission service abroad, and not merely for mission service abroad, but for mission service in a comparatively untried and difficult field. He was quietly sounded on the subject first by myself, and afterwards by Dr. Gordon ; but though he had at first his own misgivings, very natural in the peculiar circumstances of the case, he gave no negative to the proposal which was made to him to take the matter into his solemn and prayerful consideration. Well do I remember the many communings, incidental and formal, which he had with me on the subject. He made many anxious inquiries about the duties which would be expected of him in India, and of the nature of the field which he was invited there to occupy; but he did not put a single question respecting his own support when engaged in the work of the Lord, or respecting the position in society which he might be expected to occupy in India. His decision, not hastily formed and never to be abandoned, was in favour of his going to India. His offer of service, supported by suitable testimonies and testimonials from Dr. Welsh, Mr. Brydon of Dunscore, and other fathers of the Church, was at once most thankfully and joyfully accepted by the Mission Committee. When the engagement was reported to the Christian friend with whom the proposal to establish the mission at Nágpur originated, he immediately forwarded to me the payment of the large sum which he had promised, with the interest upon it from the day he had commenced his correspondence respecting its destination. He used the following noticeable words on the occasion : " I thank the Lord that from the hour he put it into my heart to place this money at your disposal for a mission to these parts, I have had much peace of mind. I am assured that the desire which was put into my heart came from

God, and his grace has supported me throughout, and enables me to say, 'All things come of thee, and of thine own have I given thee." Another zealous friend of Indian missions,* who had been mainly instrumental in founding the German Mission to the Gonds, in the forests east of Nágpur, the majority of the members of which had been carried off by epidemic cholera, expressed himself ready to contribute liberally to the Free Church Mission at Nágpur on the understanding that it should employ as Assistant Missionaries the two survivors, which was readily agreed to. Thus the cry was very distinctly heard from distant and long-neglected Nágpur, "Come over and help us."

Mr. Hislop's license as a preacher of the Gospel took place in the early part of 1844 ; and he was ordained by the Free Presbytery of Edinburgh to the office of the holy ministry as a missionary to India on the 5th September of the same year. On this occasion I was called to preside, and conduct the services, the discourses and addresses connected with which are published in my little work entitled " The Evangelization of India." The season was one of peculiar interest and solemnity to Mr. Hislop, who enjoyed in connexion with it the sympathy and prayers of many warm and attached friends. About the same time he was united in marriage to a help every way meet for him—the pious and amiable daughter of the Rev. Mr. Hull, a minister of the Church of England, and granddaughter, by her mother's side, of Erasmus Middleton, whose Evangelical Biography is well known.

Mr. and Mrs. Hislop, along with a Christian friend

---

* D. F. McLeod, C. B.

destined to assist in the Female School operations of our
mission in Puná, left Southampton for Bombay in the
beginning of November 1844 ; and, without their com-
panion, who had been taken ill on the voyage, they arrived on the 13th of the following month in Bombay,
where they received a cordial welcome. The same esti-
mate was here made of Mr. Hislop's qualifications for
missionary work that had been formed in Scotland. Mr.
Nesbit thus expressed his judgment of these qualifications :—" It would appear that in the selection of
Mr. Hislop, you have indeed enjoyed the guidance and
blessing of the Great Head of the Church. His established piety, his enlightened zeal, his calm 'and steady
purpose and patience, his sweet disposition and temper, his
powerful intellect, and his habits of substantial thought and
strict reasoning, mark him out as peculiarly fitted, not only
for missionary work in general, but for commencing
and carrying on the operations of a new and untried
sphere. His early departure, and that of his amiable
wife, both Mrs. Nesbit and myself very much regret.
They purpose leaving this on the 2nd of January."

Before starting for Nágpur, on the day here mentioned, Mr. Hislop thus recorded his own spiritual impressions and aspirations connected with his arrival in India,
and the great work in which he expected to be engaged :—" This day brings me to the commencement of a
new year; and this land, to which, through the goodness of the Almighty, I have been led in safety, is to
me a new scene. Oh! may my heart be renewed more
and more! Many and clear are the intimations I have
received that I have been brought here by the hand of
the Most High—intimations which were begun in my
native country, but which have been continued during

my voyage, and since its termination; and it becomes me therefore solemnly to consider the obligations under which I am thereby laid to give myself unto the Lord, and then to his service in connection with the spiritual welfare of my heathen neighbours."

Mr. (now Dr.) Murray Mitchell accompanied Mr. and Mrs. Hislop to Nágpur, to give them his kind assistance on the journey, as well as to aid them in their settlement at the head-quarters of their mission. By the way they took lessons from a Pandit who accompanied them, thus commencing as early as practicable the study of Maráthí, the language with which afterwards they had principally to deal in their general evangelistic ministrations. The party—having made a not useless digression to see the ancient Buddhist and Bráhmanical Excavations at Elora and Ajantá, which so well illustrate the creeds and customs of India, with which a missionary is daily brought in contact—arrived at Nágpur on the 22nd of February, 1845. They met with a cordial and most kind reception from the friends of the mission at that place, including its first proposer, and from the soldiers of the 21st North British Fusiliers, who were delighted to enjoy the ministrations of their countrymen in the distant part of the world to which they had been carried without any provision having been made for their pastoral care.

Mr. Hislop's usual residence in the sphere of his mission was at the British Camp of Sitábaldí, about a mile from the city of Nágpur, which, with the surrounding province, remained under the native Marathá Government till about eight years ago. Shortly after reaching the scene of his labours, however, he for some months resided at the larger camp of Kámptí, about ten miles

distant, removing to it in October 1845.* Here his first
educational labours commenced, in a school taught through
the medium of English. Writing of this school Mr.
Hislop said:—" At that time the native teacher arrived
from Bombay, who was to conduct the secular part of
our mission school, and now the institution is in active
operation. We have altogether on the roll the names
of fifty-nine pupils. Of these four are Europeans, a few
are Indo-Britons and native Christians, and the greater
part are Musalmans and Hindus. The Hindus, who
are the most numerous of all these classes, speak the
Tamul language, as do all the native Christians. All
are engaged in acquiring an English education, and all
are regularly instructed in the truths of the Christian
religion. There is much darkness of mind and hard-
ness of heart among the native community; but I trust
that God, in his own good time, may do great things for
our little seminary. At present we have no vernacular
schools, as at your other stations, from which to draft
the more promising youths for our English Institution;
but if the Lord will, we hope to be enabled to enlarge
our operations to that extent by and bye."

This school, principally consisting of camp-followers
from the South of India, has, with fluctuations such as
might have been expected, been maintained by the
mission to the present time, more for the sake of the
parties immediately connected with it than for the Nágpur province in general, in which the Maráthí-speaking

* Of Nágpur and its military appendages Mr. Hislop thus wrote in
1858 :—" Nágpur has a population of 120,000 ; Sitábaldí, one mile to
the west, of 15,000 ; and Kámptí, nine miles to the north-east, of 50,000.
The last two are military cantonments, and include a body of immigrants
from Southern India who have followed the Madras troops. Sitábaldí,
which is also the principal Civil station of the Province, has been selected
as the residence of the Missionaries."

population predominates. Writing of other services at Kámptí, Mr. Hislop said:—" Since I came over here, besides preaching to Támul Christians through an interpreter, I have had divine service on Sabbath for the Presbyterian soldiers in the Artillery school-room, the use of which has been kindly granted by Colonel Wynch for that purpose, as well as for our weekly prayer-meetings. On the last Sabbath of November, the Lord's Supper was administered in this cantonment, for the first time, according to the Presbyterian form. About thirty disciples encompassed the table of the Lord, all meeting in spirit, as I trust, with the Master of the feast. The day selected was in anticipation of the march of the Scots Fusiliers, who were under orders to proceed to the North-West Provinces of Bengal to be in readiness in the event of hostilities being commenced in the Panjáb. A small but devoted band of that corps joined in renewing their sacramental engagements of fidelity to the Captain of their salvation, according to the simple rites of their fatherland, from which they have been separated for many a long year." The public service for the soldiers at Kámptí, and also a prayer-meeting instituted for their benefit, have been maintained to the present time; one of the Missionaries going weekly from Sitábaldí to conduct them. They have all along, through the divine blessing, been productive of much good.

An English school similar to that at Kámptí was soon formed by Mr. Hislop at the smaller camp of Sitábaldí, the vernacular languages of its pupils being principally Hindustání and Támul. This school has also been maintained to the present day.

A more important seminary than either of those now mentioned, however, was the Anglo-Vernacular Institution soon formed by Mr. Hislop in the city of Nágpur, among the proper inhabitants of the province speaking the Maráthí language, the study of which (I would here remark) he zealously and successfully pursued, acquiring also at the same time considerable proficiency in Hindustání. This, the head-school of the mission, received from Mr. Hislop and those connected with him in the work of the Lord much attention. It is of the same character as the Mission Institutions at the Indian presidencies which are so well known, and the model of which was that, so remarkably blessed of God, which was founded at Calcutta by Dr. Duff in 1830. In it both the elementary and higher branches of knowledge have been taught, the latter through the medium of the English language. It is now more prosperous than ever, having been furnished with suitable buildings, according to a plan furnished by Colonel Boileau ; but all along it has been as a light shining in a dark place. From its commencement it was associated with a series of useful Maráthí schools, at first located in various parts of the city of Nágpur, but now joined with it under the same roof. In effecting the junction of the schools here alluded to, certain difficulties have been experienced. They were thus explained by Mr. Hislop in his report to the last General Assembly :—" Our own schools are aided by a Government grant, which amounts to £23 per mensem. In April last those in the city were all accommodated under one roof in the new building, which is finished, as far as regards the interior, though there is still a portico to be added to the front. As was anticipated, the scholars of our single institution in the city do not come up to the old aggregate of the separate schools there. This is chiefly owing to the small desire for education that still exists here—a desire which does not impel parents to send their children to a distance to obtain it. But there are other causes of diminution. When we received the Government grant, we imposed a fee on our pupils, small indeed, but still such an innovation as considerably to reduce their numbers. Again, when we came into friendly relations with the *chámbhárs* (dressers of skins and shoemakers esteemed a low caste) in the water controversy, a very natural result of their success in procuring the means of refreshing their bodies was to lead them to seek knowledge for the improvement of their children's minds. Thence a few of them proposed to send their boys to our new school. The principle on which our schools have been conducted from the first, has been to pay no deference to caste ; and in our classes at Kámptí and Sitábaldí, which are composed of youths of South Indian extraction, high and low stand side by side. But in Nágpur where Brahminical influence is strong—strong both to eradicate the desire for knowledge from the minds of the lower classes and to repress it, should it, in any instance be found to spring up, our principle was scarcely ever put to the test. When, however, the little *chámbhárs* were brought by their parents to our doors, consistency required us to admit them, though at the loss of many of our 'twice-born' scholars. But the loss is not to be compared, we trust, with the victory. By all these causes combined, the number of our English and Maráthí pupils in the city fell from 420 to 240. But what we lost in numbers we gained in efficiency. Now all these classes find room for orderly expansion, and are kept under constant superintendence." This judicious treatment of the question of caste, though causing, *pro tempore* at least, a loss of pupils, is much to be approved. It is a shame to the Governmental educational authorities and agents, in many parts of India, that they leave missionaries to contend with the gigantic evil single-handed.

It was some time, in consequence of the prejudices of the people, before anything could be done at Nágpur as regards female education; and the amount of success in this department of the mission has hitherto been but inconsiderable, though the children and adults forming its own wards have generally been taught to read. Mr. Hislop's last notice of this department of his mission is as follows:—" On the 18th July (1862) we revived our city girls' school, which for want of accommodation and other causes had become extinct. It is difficult for people in other parts of India to understand the obstacles in the way of female education. However, it is a cause of thankfulness to perceive progress even in this department of our work. Besides the 26 female pupils who are learning Maráthí under Mrs. Hislop, there are 13 who are acquiring English and Támul under Mrs. Cooper. Of course, in neither of our girls' schools are fees exacted. We think it a great point gained to secure their attendance without bribing them to come."

Of the great need of educational as well as of other evangelistic appliances in the province of Nágpur, the following concise statement, prepared by Mr. Hislop in 1858, bears ample testimony:—" The Free Church Mission is set down in a province with an area of 76,000 square miles, and a population of about four-and-a-half millions. The inhabitants in the western, or more cultivated part, speak Maráthí, and in the east a corrupt dialect of Hindí; while in the south a few are found to use Telugu. In the jungly tracts various aboriginal dialects prevail, which, with the exception of that spoken by the Kurkus or Moasis, may all be classed as Gondí, and bear a close affinity to Támul. Musalmans, who everywhere use their own language, constitute somewhat less than a thirtieth of the population, the aborigines a twelfth, and the remainder are Hindus. Brahmins abound in the larger towns, more especially in the city of Nágpur, where, till recently, they directed the royal conscience, and filled most of the offices of State. As might have been anticipated, caste feeling runs very high, and education is at the lowest ebb. In the capital itself, the whole number of children at school, irrespective of those under the instruction of the mission, does not exceed 900 out of a population of 120,000. In the immediate vicinity, a traveller may pass through village after village, each containing from 1,000 to 2,000 souls, without a school, almost without a reader, unless it be the Patel or headman, his clerk, or the village astrologer. Taking the metropolitan zillah as a whole, the proportion of readers is believed to be only one in every 200 of the inhabitants. If, however, we look beyond to the other four districts, where there is a large intermixture of aboriginal tribes, we find the people still more rude and illiterate. It is well known that these children of the forest have no written language of their own, and perhaps not a dozen of them have learned to read any other tongue. From observations that have been made on mission tours, it is conjectured that taking all classes of the people together, in Chándá only one in 300 is able to read, and in Bundárá and Chindwárá, one in 400. In the remaining zillah of Raipur the proportion must be still lower, as will readily be conceived when it is stated, that a colporteur of the mission, in 1856, travelled from Nágpur to its sudder or chief station, not indeed by the most frequented route, but nevertheless passing through a number of considerable villages, and throughout the whole distance of 200 miles, he saw only two schools with an aggregate attendance of 40 boys, more than half of whom have since been dispersed by the discontinuance of one of the schools. Probably one in 700 or 800 is the proportion of readers in the extensive district of Raipur." The statistical information here given may be relied on as an approximation to the facts of the case. Mr. Hislop conducted the most minute inquiries not only into the topography of the whole of the Nágpur province, but into the social and religious state of its varied tribes and tongues, including those in the most depressed condition. This was work specially worthy of a pioneer missionary. In the researches which he conducted in connexion with it, he ever manifested a spirit of pure benevolence and humanity, striving particularly to remove all injurious misunderstandings and misrepresentations. In one of the last letters which I had from him, he thus replied to an inquiry which I had addressed to him relative to a horrible charge long brought against one of the olden tribes of a district belonging to Nágpur: " I cannot delay my reply to your question regarding the reputed cannibalism of the aborigines east of Amarkantak. I had observed the account given by Lieutenant Prendergast, (in Alexander's E. I. Magazine, 1831,) and, as it has influenced the statement of many writers since, I had intended, whenever I put together all my notes on our jungle tribes to prove its inaccuracy; but I must now content myself by giving a very decided denial of its truth. Lieutenant Prendergast never witnessed an instance of cannibalism among the *Binjewárs*, or *Bunderwars*, as he writes the name; his whole proof is vague rumour, and the admission, as he supposed, of one concerned. I believe the fancied admission must have originated in non-familiarity with the native language and customs on the part of Lieutenant Prendergast. With his mind full of a foreign conclusion, he asked his native friend a question, which he intended to convey the idea whether he ate of the *flesh* of a man not a Binjewár. The Binjewár, on the contrary, with his mind full of caste pride (for such exists even in the forest) hears the words as if it were inquired whether he was in the habit of eating from the hands of any one lower than himself. Revulsion from the latter idea is more likely in India than from the former, even were the practice of cannibalism admitted. But all who have visited the east of Amarkantak, and passed through the Binjewars, assert that there is no such thing as eating of human flesh heard of or practised among them. I write this at the table at the other side of which Mr. Temple is seated. He returned from Sambalpur and Chatisgad about three weeks ago. During his tour he had frequent dealings with Binjewárs, but not one was suspected of cannibalism." The reports of the savage cruelty of the forest tribes generally originate in the hate of the higher castes contiguous, and some Europeans have only to credit these reports, without inquiry, to keep these tribes exterior to the pale of their benevolence. Well is it that the herald of the cross presents himself as the friend of both the oppressed and depressed.

Mr. Hislop's evangelistic efforts were not confined to education. In the second year of his residence at Nágpur he began to preach in the Maráthí language, the study of which he had diligently pursued from his first arrival in the country; and this he did both to children and adults, till the sudden close of his career, not only at stated times or places near his usual residence, but in the course of extensive and frequent itineracies, undertaken principally in the cold season.* He delighted publicly and widely to proclaim the Gospel message to all classes of the natives of India; and he derived much encouragement from his missionary journeyings, as well as from his regular local services. In the course of these journeyings he distributed (often by sale) large numbers of copies and portions of the scriptures, and religious tracts, in various languages, which he received principally from Bombay and Madras. His teaching and his preaching he found admirably to harmonize together, and to prove auxiliary to one another. His friends, who knew and appreciated his talents and acquirements, sometimes regretted that he did not attempt authorship in the native languages. Had he been nearer to a native press than he was, the case might have been otherwise.

Mr. Hislop's discourses, both in English and the native languages, were thoroughly scriptural, and sound because they were scriptural. They were the result of much meditation, thought, study, and prayer; and they were very carefully constructed and arranged. They were full of important and edify-

---

* In 1858, Mr. Hislop thus wrote respecting this department of mission work :—" The Word of Life is made known every Lord's Day to the Tamil Christians of Kámptí and Sitábaldí by catechists, and by the missionaries through their interpretation, while Mr. Hislop and Mr. Baba on alternate Sabbaths preach to the converts using that language. Every Sabbath morning a meeting for prayer and exposition of the scripture in Maráthí is held, for lack of better accommodation, in the shade of the mission-house, where from 200 to 300 scholars regularly assemble from the city. Opportunities are embraced during the week, of preaching to adults in the city, while visiting the vernacular schools ; and a month is usually spent every year in proclaiming the Gospel in the villages around."

ing matter, expressed in plain, but appropriate and for-
cible, language. They were delivered more in a deli-
berate and solemn, than in a fluent and energetic manner.
Yet they secured the attention of his hearers, and were
eminently profitable. Both the more intelligent and the
less intelligent classes of his hearers found in them a
word in season. It was evident to all that he did not
stand up in the pulpit, or in the place of public concourse,
to glorify himself, but to glorify his great Master.
With mere rhetorical art and finesse he had no sympathy.
The sincerity and honesty which he manifested in private
life, he carried into the pulpit; and the calm and peace-
ful earnestness which he manifested in the pulpit he
carried into private life.

Both in teaching and preaching Mr. Hislop early
received both valuable assistance and co-operation.
" The German brethren" (associated with him on his
arrival at Nágpur, he wrote) " were the survivors
of a Gond mission commenced at Amarkantak, which,
in the mysterious providence of God, had lost its
other four members by disease in the course of a week.
Those simple pious men, however, were not long spared
to labour at their new station. In August 1845, Mr.
Bartels, after giving promise of much usefulness, was
called to his rest, and in May 1848, he was followed by
his devoted countryman Mr. Apler." In 1847 he received an able colleague from Scotland, the Rev. Robert
Hunter, M. A., who was altogether congenial to him in
his religious views and feelings, literary and scientific
attainments, and Christian sympathy and affection. Mr.
Hunter remained with him, faithfully labouring in the
different departments of mission work, till his health
failed him in 1855, when he returned to his native coun-

try. He was succeeded by the Rev. J. G. Cooper, who had had two years' experience of missionary labour in our flourishing mission at Madras, and who has proved entirely of a kindred spirit, faithfully devoting his energies to the work of the Lord. When in 1858, Mr. Hislop proceeded to Europe (where he remained for two years) for the benefit of his health, his place was occupied by the devoted Rev. Adam White, M. A., and afterwards by the Rev. Richard Stothert, M A., whom we have the valued privilege of now having with us in our mission in Bombay. To the native agents, graciously raised up by the Lord at Nágpur, I shall immediately allude.

Mr. Hislop and his colleagues did not long labour at Nágpur, without witnessing the divine blessing, in its higher form, rest on both their general evangelistic and educational efforts and enterprizes. The cases of conversion which from time to time he has reported have, in some instances, been of a specially interesting character. The first of these was that of Jádavají, the Patel, or headman, of the village of Vishnur. Writing of him to myself in December 1847, he said :—"He is an excellent man, very shrewd, and well educated considering his privileges. He has a wonderful knowledge of the scriptures, and I believe they are within his heart. Still, having been brought up in a village, and spent in it a life of upwards of sixty years, he has many habits which would be better wanting ; and which do not mar the character and habits of your young and well-trained converts. The chief defect is an inability and perhaps a slight disinclination to communicate what he knows to others. If left to himself he would read and pray all the day, and enjoying the sweets of religion himself, he would make little effort to extend them. However, we hope that when he gets into the villages, and meets with men to whose habits and manners he is accustomed he will show greater self-denial and activity." This expectation was happily realised. Of several domestic servants who had been led to embrace the truth as it is in Jesus, he expressed a very favourable opinion. Of one of them he said, " He evidently feels much of the power of true religion, and he adorns his profession by an honest and faithful discharge of his duties as unto the Lord." Of another he wrote, " He is a respectable scholar in his own language (Telugu), and is well acquainted with the popular Hindu books. While these were the only subjects of his study he had no consciousness of sin, as he found that the conduct which was most agreeable to his own inclinations was attributed in the Rámáyana and other such works to the gods whom he was taught to revere and obey. The first book of a different tendency which he perused with attention was a copy of the Indian Pilgrim, which he received from the Nágpur mission. He there learned for the first time the nature of the Gospel; but still salvation was not desired until he was made to feel his sinfulness by comparing his life with the requirements of the divine law as contained in the book of Exodus. Convinced now by the word of God of his need of a Saviour, the knowledge which he had derived from the tract recurred to his mind with an unusual feeling of suitableness and power. Then it was, as he himself states, that he was constrained to give himself up to the Saviour, and to solicit baptism according to Christ's command." A young, but intelligent, Bráhman pupil of the Nágpur Institution, who had there and at the missionhouse received much instruction, professed his attachment to the cause of Christ before he was " of age" according to the Hindu law, and threw himself upon the protection of Mr. Hislop. The Nágpur Rájá (on the application of his father) demanded his extradition as a minor; and the Acting British Resident at the native court, according to the interpretation which he put on the treaty with that court, ordered his delivery to the native authorities, without entering into questions respecting the youth's discretion, or, in the first instance at least, seeking for guarantees as to his humane treatment. The consequence was, that the youth, adhering to his convictions, was imprisoned by the Rájá for nearly four months. He seemed to have been guilty of some concession to heathenism when he obtained his liberty ; but for this, ere long, in the mercy of God, he became penitent, and returned to the mission, where, after further instruction and due probation, he was baptized. He has now for many years evinced the sincerity and strength of his religious convictions by a walk and conversation becoming the Gospel. These cases I allude to as specimens of the work of conversion, effected under the ministry of Mr. Hislop and his associates at Nágpur. That all the others which there occurred were equally satisfactory, however promising at first they might be in the eyes of Christian charity, I am not able to say. Neither have I any warrant to make any insinuation to the contrary. Missionaries, as is to be expected, have their trials with their flocks as well as ministers dealing with the hereditary profession of Christianity in highly favoured Christendom. In Mr. Hislop's last Report, the number of 'natives admitted into the church at Nágpur on their own profession of faith in Jesus is stated at sixty-one. The number of full communicants at the date of that document (March,

1863) was forty-five, including some from other stations ; the number of baptized adherents not communicants was forty-one, and of baptized children fifty-four, making a total of one hundred and forty of Native Christians under the charge of the Mission, forming a body of professors of our holy faith in an interesting position in this great country, the steady increase of which by the divine blessing, may be reasonably expected, if the Nágpur Mission be vigorously supported.

In the body of Christians here alluded to, several suitable Christian agents, raised up by divine providence, have been found. Two of them, including Mr. Bábá Pandurang, who suffered imprisonment at the hands of the native Rájá at the first commencement of his Christian course, and his friend Mr. V. Rámaswámi, have, after going through an extensive course of general and theological instruction, been licensed as Preachers of the Gospel by the Free Presbytery of Bombay. One is a Catechist, also acting as a teacher ; eight, including one studying for the ministry, and another, who is a Scripture Reader, are Teachers. One, Apaya, an early convert, is a Colporteur. In connexion with the duties of the last mentioned agent and other Christian brethren occasionally associated with him, the following interesting and judicious statements and suggestions are from the pen of Mr. Hislop himself :—" Colportage is no unimportant department of the work at Nágpur. Carried on in and around the mission stations throughout the whole year, it is extended during the cold season and part of the hot weather to the utmost limits of the Province, and not unfrequently into the adjacent territory of the Nizám. Thus on an average as many as 5,000 copies of the Word of God and religious tracts and books, realizing about

Rs. 300, are annually disposed of, in Támul and Telugu, and in Maráthí, Hindí and Urdu, as well as English. The vernacular works in number amount to seven-eighths of the whole, though they bring only one-fourth of the price. The Colporteurs while selling take occasion also to preach. Frequently interesting incidents occur. This year one of these agents penetrated into the Hyderabad country as far as Mahadevapur on the Godávarí. In a secluded village named Yidilawárá he met a Telugu woman of the cowherd caste, who not only could read herself, but was engaged in teaching her younger brother the valued art. Such was her love of learning, that in the absence of money she took off from her arm the only silver bangle which she wore, and, having had it cut in two, gave one of the pieces for some portions of the Telugu Scriptures which she had selected. A great part of the following night she spent in conversation with the Colporteur on the meaning of various passages which she had at once begun to peruse. The number of Christian publications now circulated by sale throughout Nágpur and the neighbouring districts is more than equal to the gratuitous distribution formerly effected on tours, while there is no comparison between the two systems in regard to the feeling of satisfaction with which the books are put into circulation. By the present mode, mendicancy, which in this land has been exalted into a religious profession, is resisted ; the spirit of dependence, which animates all classes, and even enters the Christian Church, is discouraged ; and, for every book that is distributed, the receiver furnishes the surest pledge of which the case admits, that it shall be preserved, read, and valued. The plan, which is here cordially recommended to all who have not yet tested it, is no local experiment, for it has been adopted throughout the Bombay Presidency. It is no novelty, the working of which remains to be seen, but it is an established practice, followed by the missionaries of Western India for the last ten years, and fully realising their most sanguine expectations.* In the experience of the Nágpur mission, which has to do with people speaking Támil, as well as those using Maráthí, it has been found equally applicable to both ; and if only brethren in the south were to agree to give it a trial for two or three years, little doubt need be entertained that the evils resulting from the long continuance of the opposite system would be surmounted, and the change would be attended by the most beneficial consequences."

In all his intercourse with the people of India, I would now remark, Mr. Hislop had ever a benevolent and Christian aim, directed by the soundest judgment. He ever sought to make good impressions on the minds of all with whom he was conversing, or whom he was instructing, in the house, in the school, in the church, on the road, on the street, or in the fields. He was careful to mark any favourable symptoms which might make their appearance in those whom he addressed, and he was peculiarly attentive to religious inquirers, giving them personal instructions and advice, directing their reading, and recommending them to hold communion with those likely to do them good. He was, in an important sense, the mainspring of the native agency of the mission, counselling and

---

* Since 1832, when the " First Exposure of Hinduism," for which there was a great demand among the natives, appeared, the plan of selling at least some publications and tracts, in a few instances even at their full cost price, has been acted on by one or two of the Bombay missionaries. The publications of the Bombay Tract and Book Society are, as a rule, sold at reduced prices. An advance on some of these might now be reasonably made.

encouraging its members to the full extent of his power, and regarding all parties, whatever their position might be, with attention and favour. The consequence of all this was, that he was universally loved and esteemed, and exercised a salutary influence far and wide.

A similar remark may be made respecting the power for good which Mr. Hislop uniformly exercised among all classes of Europeans, and particularly those connected with the military and civil establishments of this land, who formed the majority of our countrymen with whom he held intercourse. While seeking the Christianization of the natives of India, he could not view with indifference the dechristianization (alas! too frequent in this remote land) of those who were bone of his bone and flesh of his flesh, from the highly-favoured Isles of Britain. All Europeans coming within his reach, he sought, and often not without success, to make even auxiliaries (by their prayers, contributions and efforts) in the evangelistic enterprize. His public preachings, his more private recommendations and expositions of the divine word at Bible meetings and family parties, his genial and instructive conversations in the ordinary intercourse of life, his exemplary temper and conduct, and his valuable and extensive correspondence, will long be remembered with gratitude and profit by hundreds. His spirit was eminently catholic, and could give no just offence to evangelical Christians of any denomination. By chaplains and bishops like-minded with himself, he was viewed as a brother and fellow-labourer, with whom they had pleasure in co-operating.*

---

* The following is Mr. Hislop's last notice of the operations of the Nágpur mission among our countrymen :—" For them we conduct a

The influence of Mr. Hislop among Europeans in Central India was often extended and maintained by his high scientific attainments and interesting researches, particularly connected with geology. In the neighbourhood of Nágpur, where several remarkable formations unite, some interesting pages of the book of nature connected with the olden world lie exposed to view ; and these (which had more or less attracted the attention of other naturalists) Mr. Hislop, after much attention study, and inquiry, was able to decipher and expound, both in an intelligent and truthful spirit, and in such a way as to secure the interest and sympathy of other competent observers, not only at Nágpur, but throughout India, and even in Europe. The fruits of his researches appear in several able papers in the Journal of the Bombay Branch of the Royal Asiatic Society, and of the Proceedings and Journal of the Geological Society. The most important of them is one " On the Geology and Fossils of the Neighbourhood of Nágpur," in preparing

week-day and a Sabbath service in each of the two European stations of Sitábaldí and Kámptí. Last month we bade adieu to H. M.'s 91st Regiment, which has been stationed in our province for the last four years. To that period some of the men will look back eternally as the season when they found the Saviour. One who confessed his Lord for the first time here, is now on his way to Rájputáná to join our United Presbyterian brethren as a Catechist. He promises to be a workman that needeth not to be ashamed. The 91st has been succeeded by the 1st Royals, which being an English corps does not contain so many Presbyterians as the other. Nor are there so many who follow the Captain of Salvation. However, there are a few warm-hearted Christians, who meet regularly for prayer among themselves, and with them, though for the most part members of the Episcopal Church, we count it a pleasure to meet, when we go on Saturday evening to Kámptí. For the head-quarters of the regiment there, the prayer-house opened last year is found to be a most suitable place of spiritual retirement for the detachment stationed here. My house has been opened as a retreat for an hour from the noise of the barracks, and for reading the word and prayer."

which he had the able co-operation of his colleague, Mr.
Hunter, like himself an accomplished naturalist; and
another "On the Tertiary Deposits associated with Trap-
Rock in the East Indies, with descriptions of the Fossil
Shells." This is not the place to state in detail the varied
findings of these valuable scientific memoirs.* An attentive perusal of these must show to every reader that
they bear the impression of high talent and accomplish-
ment; and that much thought and time must have
been spent in their elaboration. Was this expenditure
of talent and opportunity of action, justifiable in the case
of a missionary, whose main business is with man needing the salvation of God? This question, Mr. Hislop
told me, he had often seriously put to himself, answering
it in the affirmative. The **study** of the works of God,
in their own measure, he found to be refreshing to his
own mind, exhausted by other occupations, and nutritive
of his own piety, feeling, as he must have done, that what
is worthy of God to create is worthy of man to behold.
For his ability and acquirements in natural history,
he felt himself responsible, as for the other talents com-
mitted to his charge. In their use he found he could
exercise a beneficial influence on all his fellow-students
of nature with whom he was privileged to associate
and communicate. The results of his researches he
found to be subservient to truth, and consequently
glorifying to the God of truth. Some of them he used
to explode local pretensions and superstitions of an
injurious character. Geology was to him what Botany
was to the venerable and devoted Dr. Carey—his pas-
time in the more serious business of life. The fear of
geological pursuits cherished in certain minds on the

---

* See Note A in the Appendix.

supposition of their hostility to the Divine Scriptures is altogether groundless and unreasonable, for the utmost harmony must exist between the Book of Nature and the Book of Revelation, though man may err in the rightful interpretation of the one or the other. In the writings of Moses we find announced the great fact, so widely and long forgotten by the nations of the earth, that " In the beginning God created the heaven and earth"; and that creation, the product of God's unlimited wisdom and power, had its order and sequences, " For in six days the LORD made heaven and earth, the sea and all that in them is, and rested the seventh day." How do the discoveries of geology testifying to the existence of the world for ages of incalculable duration, and to repeated creations, in their course, of vegetables and animals, the remains of which are still to be found embedded in the crust of the earth, affect the general question of an authoritative revelation from God founded on miraculous testimony? They tell us that since every creation is a miracle, and that as there have been many miraculous forthputtings of the divine power in fitting the world for the abode of man, there can be no difficulty in supposing that miraculous interpositions were continued after the formation of man, for his instruction in the nature and responsibility of his position as the lord of the world on which he dwelt, and the intelligent and ministering priest of the visible universe by which he was surrounded; and that even after he had fallen from his holy and happy state by the transgression of revealed law, God may have actually condescended to hold direct intercourse with him, in order to make known to him a scheme of salvation by a Redeemer, and maintain him and his believing descendants in a state of allegiance to him as the

God both of mercy and holiness.* What do they (combined with those of Astronomy) with the intimations of change and even decay, which they furnish, but give emphasis to the humble, but sublime, praise of the Psalmist :—

> Of old hast thou laid the foundations of the earth :
> And the heavens are the work of thy hands.
> They shall perish, but thou shalt endure :
> Yea all of them shall wax old as a garment ;
> As a vesture shalt thou change them, and they shall be changed ;
> But thou art the same, and thy years shall have no end.

What does the enlargement of our ideas of the six days, or creative epochs with their morn and eve, encouraged by geology (though it cannot yet mark the beginning and end of even the characteristic and distinguishing products of some of these epochs), but give emphasis to the impressive declaration, that " One day is with the Lord as a thousand years, and a thousand years as one day" ; and give power to the voice of the Eternal Wisdom, making the majestic proclamation which we see in the eighth chapter of Proverbs, in which we find a progressive creation, with what may be long intervals, distinctly alluded to :—

> I was set up from everlasting
> From the beginning, or ever the earth was.
> When there were no depths I was brought forth :
> When there were no fountains abounding with water.
> Before the mountains were settled :
> Before the hills was I brought forth :
> While as yet he had not made the earth nor the fields,
> Nor the highest (elementary) part of the dust of the earth.

If God still refrains from creative work, and his Sabbath still continues since his last creative action connected with our system, what may have been the measure of his working days but such great ages as geology indicates ? Geology, enlarging our vision with its glimpses into the vista of the past, and yet losing itself in the immensity

---

* See " Star of Bethlehem" by the Author.

behind it, and showing everywhere the powerful working of the agencies of fire and flood, ordained and directed by God, leads us devoutly to exclaim,

> Lo, these are parts of his ways
> But how little a portion is heard of him ?
> But the thunder of his power who can understand ?

In the prosecution of his varied missionary labours,
Mr. Hislop had his distinctive trials. While he
bore the name of the Lord before the Gentiles
and Kings, it was shown to him as to Saul of Tarsus,
how great things he should suffer for his name's
sake. He had several severe attacks of illness, connected especially with Indian fever, one of which drove him
to his native country for a couple of years, commencing
with the close of 1858. He was bit, in several parts of
the lower extremities of his body, by a rabid dog, to the
great alarm of his family and friends. He was greatly
distressed by the surrender to the tender mercies of an
unenlightened government the young Bráhman convert
to whom we have already alluded, and to find that he
was forcibly deprived of his liberty, and kept in confine-
ment for many weeks. His house was broken into by a
mob, when another inquirer took refuge in it, the as-
sault on that occasion being so violent that a considerable fine was inflicted on the native government for its
connivance in the case. He was nearly killed by another mob in the city of Nágpur, having been mistaken
for a political agent, expected to carry into effect some
necessary measure displeasing to the supporters of the
native administration, which had terminated soon after
the death of the Bhonslé Rájá in 1854. During the
continuation of the native administration he was greatly
grieved by the salutes fired by our troops nominally to
H. Highness's honour when he appeared in public at na-

tive heathen festivals. Respecting this matter, he thus wrote to me, " I should despair of convincing the natives that the honours paid to their princes on their religious festivals are mere royal salutes. So long as the British Government pay their respect to a Hindu Rájá only on the day of Ráma or Ganésha, or any other heathen holiday, and omit their compliments on every other day of the year, so long will they believe that they choose the day not on account of the King, but in respect of the occasion." When the native government passed away, he was no less grieved to find merely discretional grants, given to Hindu temples, continued as under a heathen administration. Though not willing that any encouragement should be given in any form to native error and superstition, he was much respected and beloved for his benevolence and beneficence by the native community. It was to him that in the sad year of 1857, a plot to destroy the Europeans of Nágpur was revealed; and it was through the information thus given to him, that, in the goodness of God, that catastrophe was averted. He faithfully followed the Lord through good report and through bad report.

Though Mr. Hislop ever did full justice to the British authorities at Nágpur in his communications to his friends, he expressed particular delight with remarkable improvements, which began to appear in the administration of the province in 1862. Writing to me on the 27th of August of that year, he said, " In Captain Dods, the head of the (Educational) Department, your Presidency has furnished us apparently with an excellent man. Our Chief Commissioner is another Sir Bartle Frere for the friendly interest which he takes in mission education, and in every plan for the good of the people. I have seldom seen a man like Mr. Temple for energy of body and activity of mind. His Administrative Report recently submitted to Government is a most comprehensive one, but it was required, being actually the first on Nágpur since the annexation. We have made an application for grants-in-aid to the extent of Rs. 240 per mensem. I think it will be conceded. Mr. T. sees the propriety of establishing no Government school in Nágpur city, where we have one, and where the desire for education is still small. He has also to a certain extent reversed the order for the exclusion of Maráthí from the Courts. He is seeking his information from all quarters, and forming his plans after mature deliberation." When writing his Report for the last General Assembly, he said, " The past year has been one of marked material progress in this province. The arrival of Mr. Temple has in this respect been a signal blessing." In illustration of this remark he noticed " the prohibition of self-inflicted torture in the worship of idols," in hook-swinging, and body-piercing by swords; the " abolition of caste-distinctions in drawing water from public tanks and wells ;" the restoration of the vernacular Maráthí to use in the courts of Nágpur ; and the extension of (liberal) grants-in-aid (in compliance with the famous Despatch of Sir Charles Wood of 1854) to the schools of the mission.

But we must now draw this discourse and imperfect narrative to a close. A greater loss in the Indian Mission field could scarcely have been sustained by us than that which has occurred in the sudden and unexpected death of our dearly beloved brother STEPHEN HISLOP, just when he had reached the very zenith of his influence and usefulness in Central India, and the highest hopes,—founded on his exemplary and exalted charac-

ter, his unreserved and untiring devotedness to the
evangelistic enterprize, his sound and sober and enlightened judgment, his high scientific attainments and discoveries, his affectionate attachment to the fruits of his
own ministry and of his fellow-labourers in the Gospel of
Christ, and the respect and esteem with which he was
universally regarded by all who knew him,—were cherished respecting his advancement in his noble career.
That loss, however, has been ordered and effected by God
himself ; and in the view of it we must humble ourselves
under his sovereign and powerful hand. We must do
more than this in connexion with this sore affliction and
great bereavement. We must consider the purposes
which in the all-wise and holy providence of God it is
fitted to subserve. It is certainly a loud call for those
of us who are still spared in this great field of India, yet
so little regarded, to abound more and more in the work
of the Lord, and for the friends of missions at home to
seek and to send without delay new auxiliaries to fill up
and extend our broken and limited ranks. Let us most
anxiously and prayerfully seek the improvement of the
affliction which has befallen us, lest the strokes of the
Lord's displeasure,—administered in wisdom, love, and
faithfulness, but marking judgment as well as mercy,—be
multiplied upon us both in Heathendom and Christendom.
Let us at the same time acknowledge and feel that our
public loss is the gain of our departed brother personally
considered, and the gain of that heaven, the expanding
treasure-house of God's holy ones, into which he has
entered. In the providence of God he was doubtlessly
prepared for the change which so suddenly awaited him.*

---

* For an interesting account of Mr. Hislop's last hours, see Appendix B.

Precious in the sight of the Lord was the death of this saint, though it was not marked by human eye. It was the hand of the loving Saviour which received the spirit of the departing one, and now that spirit is with the Lord. A Christian loses his life, when his days are completed according to the will of God ; but he loses not his soul. He loses not his title to eternal life, which is the purchase and gift of his Lord and Saviour. He loses not his moral nature, which has been renewed and sanctified by the Holy Spirit. He loses not his heaven-bestowed capacity of enjoying and glorifying God. When his flesh and heart faileth, he finds GOD the strength of his heart and his portion for ever. When he leaves the earth he goes to heaven, where, without measure, he enjoys the fruition of God.

We must all admit that our dear departed brother was a God-formed and a God-given evangelist. Let us all praise God for his original power and talents, and educational culture; for his call to the family and church of God; for his thorough preparation for the Christian ministry; for his commission and appointment to the high-places of the field; for the blessings vouchsafed to him and through him when engaged in the work of the Lord; and for the fruits of his service, and the savour of his example which he has left behind. To that Lord and Master who formed and gave him, let us look, if not now for apostles and prophets, yet for evangelists, pastors, and teachers, "for the perfecting of the saints (both in number and character) for (or, towards) the work of the ministry, for the edifying of the body of Christ : till we all come in the unity of the faith, and of the knowledge of the Son of God, unto a perfect man, unto the measure of the stature of the fulness of Christ."

7

While we honour God for his gifts let us pray for their increase. Let us do this especially in the view of the wants of India (with its two hundred millions of inhabitants), which we have not yet, with any degree of adequacy, been taken into the practical consideration of even benevolent Christians. In this great country, there is an almost immeasurable field, yet unbroken, nay, covered with pestilential and poisonous growths of ages of error, delusion, superstition, fanaticism, and immorality; while in the comparatively few spots that have been partially cleared and cultivated, a most promising harvest is beginning to appear. Let us then pray to him who is alike the Lord of "the field which is the world," and the Lord of the harvest yet to be reaped from the wide extent of that field, to raise up and send forth labourers into his harvest. Those who have been already provided, and so many of whom have already fallen even on the high places of the field, are surely earnests of good things to come in this matter. Let all waiting the call of the Lord to his own ministry be very attentive to that call when it may be addressed to them in the divine providence; and let them be ready to carry the Gospel message to the very ends of the earth, believing that the place of duty, however remote and trying, is the place of spiritual safety and privilege. Let those who perhaps cannot work be so ready to give, as that all our missionary churches, societies, and institutions, shall be able to say (like the American Board of Commissioners for Foreign Missions on its fiftieth anniversary) that they have found the means of sending to, and supporting in the heathen world, all candidates for missionary employment who have appeared to them really fit for the discharge of its duties. The woes and wants of India, more than those of Macedonia of old, send forth the piercing and affecting cry, COME OVER AND HELP US. Unhappy indeed are those who lend a deaf year to that cry; and who disregard the plain and authoritative command of the risen and exalted Saviour, GO YE AND DISCIPLE ALL NATIONS. Blessed are those who, obeying that command, die in the Lord from henceforth: Yea, saith the Spirit, that they may rest from their labours; and their works do follow them.

APPENDIX.

(A) NOTE ON THE RESULTS OF
MR. HISLOP'S GEOLOGICAL RESEARCHES.

In the paper " On the Geology and Fossils of the Neighbourhood of Nágpur,"[*] Mr. Hislop takes a general view of the Physical Geography of the District; gives a history of the geological observations made in it; classifies and describes its rock formations; notices its superficial strata; and refers to its fossils and minerals, which are more particularly described by Mr. Hunter. He thus sums up the results of his researches :—

" In tracing the geological history of this district from the facts that have been brought forward, we are made to feel that the early epochs are involved in the utmost obscurity. While in many other countries the records of what took place in Palœozoic times have been preserved in successive strata of the earth's crust, in the Dakhan they have been wholly obliterated. It is not until we come down to the Jurassic era that we meet with archives whose characters can be read. Then we find that Central India was covered by a large body of fresh water, which stretched southward into the Peninsula, and eastward into Bengal, while on the north and west it communicated by some narrow channel with the sea. On the shores of this lake earth-worms crawled, and small reptiles (frogs) crept over the soft mud. In its pools sported flocks of little Entomostracans resembling the modern Estheria, mingled with which were Ganoid fishes and Labyrinthodonts.[†] The streams which fed it brought down into its bed the debris of the Plutonic and Metamorphic rocks which then constituted the greater part of the dry land, and which were covered with an abundant vegeta-

---

[*] This paper, which appears in the Geological Journal, Vol. XI., is reprinted by H. J. Carter, F. R. S., in his " Geological Papers on Western India."

[†] For an interesting account, by Professor Owen, of a Labyrinthodont (*Brachyops Laticeps*), obtained by Messrs. Hislop and Hunter at Mangalí, sixty miles south of Nágpur, see the *Geological Journal*, Vol. XI., and Mr. Carter's " Geological Papers on Western India," pp. 288-301.

tion of Ferns,* most of them distinguished by the entireness of their fronds. Low-growing plants with grooved and jointed stems inhabited the marshes ; and Conifers and other Dicotyledonous trees, with Palms, raised their heads aloft. Meanwhile Plutonic action was going on, and strata, as they were formed, were shattered and reconstructed into a breccia ; and finally an extensive outburst of granite elevated the bed of the lake and left it dry land. The sea now flowed at Pondicherry and Trichinopoly, depositing the cretaceous strata which are found there.

" At the end of this epoch Central India suffered a depression, and was again covered by a vast lake, communicating with the sea, not towards Cutch as before, but in the neighbourhood of Rájámandarí, to which the salt water had now advanced. When the lake had during its appointed time furnished an abode to its peculiar living creatures and plants, it was invaded by an immense outpouring of trap, which filled up its bed, and left Western and a greater part of Central India a dreary waste of lava. But these basaltic steppes were ere long broken up. A second eruption of trap, not now coming to the surface, but forcing a passage for itself under the newer lacustrine strata, lifted up the superincumbent mass in ranges of flat-topped hills. Since then, to the east, water has swept over the plutonic and sandstone rocks, and laid down quantities of transported materials impregnated with iron, and some time after there were deposited in the west a conglomerate, imbedding bones of huge mammals ; and above it a stratum of brown clay, which immediately preceded the superficial deposits of the black and red soils."

The title of the last of Mr. Hislop's papers indicates its contents :— " On the Tertiary Deposits associated with Trap-Rock, in the East Indies, with Descriptions of the Fossil Shells." Notes on the Fossil Insects by Andrew Murray, F. R. S. E., and on Fossil Cypridæ, by T. Rupert Jones, F. G. S., are added to it.

Before treating of the Fossil Shells which form the bulk of Mr. Hislop's text, he notices two minerals from the immediate neighbourhood of Nágpur. These, when examined and carefully analysed by Professor Haughton of Dublin, have been found to be new to science. One of them, that accomplished chemist and mineralogist has denominated *Hislopite ;* and the other *Hunterite.* In the Hislopite, Professor Haughton found " a remarkable combination of calcareous matter, which gives the outward form to the whole crystal, with a grass-green silici-

---

* A valuable and beautiful collection by Mr. Hislop of some of these Ferns is to be found in the Museum of the Bombay Branch of the Royal Asiatic Society.

ous skeleton of glauconite, which, on analysis, he finds to be a hydrated tersilicate of protoxide of iron," or, in more technical form :—

$$\begin{matrix} 3 \ R \ O \\ Al \ ^2 \ O \ ^3 \end{matrix} \Big\} \quad 3 \ Si \ O \ ^3 + 3 \ H \ O.$$

The Hunterite, neglecting the lime and magnesia in it, which are inconsiderable, is found to consist " of five atoms of a hydrated tersilicate of alumina, combined with one atom of a hyaline silica of admitted composition."—or

$$5 \ [\ Al \ ^2 \ O \ ^3 , \ 3 \ Si \ O \ ^3 \ + \ 3 \ HO \ ]+[\ HO \ 3 \ Si \ O \ ^3 \ ]$$

After noticing the sites of the fossil shells, extending even to Rájámandarí (at the apex of the delta of the Godávarí) on the S. E. coast of the peninsula, Mr. Hislop describes first the new species (and in three instances more distinct examples than those formerly seen) of *Fossil Freshwater Shells from the Nágpur Province;* associating with them the names of some of his scientific and literary friends. They are the following :—

Melania, Hunteri ; *Paludina,* normalis, Deccanensis *(Sowerby),* Wapsharei, acicularis, Pyramis, subcylindracea, Sankeyi, Taklienses, soluta, conoidea, Rawesi, Virapai ; *Valvata,* minima, unicaranifera, multicarinata, decollata, Nagpurensis ; *Limnæ,* oviformis, subulata *(Sow.)* attenuata, Telankhediensis (3 var.) Spina ; *Physa,* Prinsepii (Sow.), normalis (3 var.) ; *Unio,* Malcolmsoni, (discovered by Dr. Malcolmson, but named by Mr. H.) Deccanensis, Hunteri, mamillatus, imbricatus, Carteri. He then describes thirty-six new species of *Fossil Estuarine Shells from Rájámandarí :*—*Fusus,* pygmæus ; *Pseudoliva;* elegans; *Natica,* Stoddardi ; *Cerithium,* multiforme, subcylindraceum, Leithii, Stoddardi ; *Vicarya,* fusiformis ; *Turritella,* prælonga ; *Hydrobia,* Ellioti, Carteri, Bradleyi; *Hemitoma ?* multiradiata ; *Ostrea,* Pangadiensis ; *Anomia,* Kateruensis (3 var.) ; *Perna,* meleagrinoides ; *Arca,* striatula ; *Nucula,* pusilla ; *Lucina,* parva, Kellia ? nana ; *Corbis,* elliptica ; *Corbicula,* ingens; *Cardita,* variabilis, pusilla ; *Cytherea,* Wilsoni, Wapsharei, Rawesi, Jerdoni, elliptica, Hunteri ; *Tellina,* Woodwardi; *Psamobia,* Jonesi ; *Cordula,* Oldhami, sulcifera. He concludes by noticing two new *fossil shells from the Narbadá,* the *Bulimus* Oldhamianus, and the *Pisidium* Medlicottianum. The principal value of all these shells is found in their use as historical *documenta.* Their testimony is that on which Mr. Hislop much relies in his judgment of the comparative age of the rocks in which they appear.

From the thirteen specimens of *Fossil Insects* placed in his hands by Mr. Hislop, Mr. Murray infers that " the Entymological Fauna of Nágpur, at the era of these fossils, was probably smaller than that of the present day;" and that they point more to a warm climate than a temperate one.

Mr. Rupert Jones, F. G. S., describing the Fossil Cypridæ procured by Messrs. Hislop and Hunter, from the neighbourhood of Nágpur, notices their large variety, and the perfect preservation of their carapaces. The specimens of these Cypridæ presented by Mr. Hislop to myself in Bombay, are so minute that only the eye of an experienced naturalist could have discerned them in the matrix in which they were found. A similar remark may be made on some of the shells, which Mr. H. describes, as the Hydrobia Ellioti, the Hydrobia Carteri, etc.

(B) LAST HOURS OF THE REV. S. HISLOP.

(Related by R. Temple, Esq., Chief Commissioner of the

Central Provinces.)

The Residency, Nágpur, September 9th, 1863.

My dear Mrs. Hislop,—In common with many other friends, I must offer to you the expression of my deep condolence in your most melancholy and sudden bereavement. At the same time, as it so happened that several of your late husband's last hours on earth were spent with me, it may be acceptable if I give you a brief account of what passed during Thursday and Friday last, the 3rd and 4th September.

Early on Thursday morning Mr. Hislop arrived at Borí from Nágpur. At Borí the party consisted of Captain Mackenzie, Lieutenant Puckle, and myself. I had a conversation with Mr. Hislop that evening before breakfast. He began by asking about the results of the new Educational System in the Wardah district, through which our party had recently been touring; and he seemed glad to hear that the several young men who had come up from Bombay to teach in the village schools were proving successful, as setting an example of progress, and at least of intellectual enlightenment. Whatever might be the right view on higher questions, he certainly thought that the State did so far well in diffusing some light among the villages in the interior of the country, which he described as sunk in the deepest ignorance. He then alluded to the Mission school in the Nágpur city, and to the grants-in-aid. I think he said that an additional teacher was expected from Scotland; that one had been advertised for, and that suitable candidates might be expected to come forward. He then adverted to the intention of the Mission to establish a new school in the Sitábaldí bázár, for which also a grant-in-aid was proposed. He said that he expected to open it very shortly, and that the only difficulty had been house-accommodation, which difficulty he had now overcome. It was remarked that when education was being diffused among the villages, something ought to be done in Sitábaldí, which was immediately under the eye of head-quarters. He then showed me several scientific and antiquarian journals illustrative of Druidical (or Scythian) remains, found alike in Great Britain and India.

After breakfast he read a chapter from the Bible to the party, and offered up a prayer. Shortly afterwards the conversation which took place was about the conversion of heathen youths. He said that Hindus were more accessible to the persuasive and convincing truth of the Gospel at an early age than at any other age; and that their consciences were then more tender and impressible. He mentioned the circumstances of the conversion of a Maráthá youth some years ago, and of the efforts, partially successful, of the parents to gain influence and authority over the youth. He said that in his father's house the youth was treated as an outcast, and relapsed into sin; that afterwards, when unquestionably a major (that is, arrived at full legal privileges) he returned to the mission. Reference was then made to the recent case of Hemnáth of Calcutta. Mr. Hislop seemed to think that the judicial opinions recently given differed from those given by Chief Justice Burton at Madras; but agreed with that of Sir Erskine Perry at Bombay (in the case of Shrípat, in his thirteenth year). He said that it would be satisfactory to missionaries in India, if it were finally decided by the highest judicial authority, as to whether or not a heathen parent could prevent his child when under age from openly professing Christianity. He thought that a child of sufficient sense and discretion might even, though under age, be allowed without any hindrance from parental authority to profess Christianity.

Being occupied I did not see him more that day, till the afternoon, when we rode out to Túkulghát, a village three miles distant from Borí. At Túkulghát we looked at a number of stone-circles of a Druidical character, and it was determined that excavations should then be made in several of these, and the next day, in search of buried remains. Returning that evening through the village of Túkul-

ghát, we met a newly-appointed village schoolmaster in company with
the landlord of the village. We spoke to the men, and told the landlord that he should give the schoolmaster all the assistance he could.
Mr. Hislop remarked that it was of consequence to raise the character
of a schoolmaster in the eyes of the natives, inasmuch as the scholastic
profession was not so highly esteemed as it ought to be by the villagers,
and in the interior. We then returned to Borí. Before the party
retired to rest that evening, Mr. Hislop offered up prayer as usual.
Thursday was spent in this way.

Early on the morning of Friday the 4th, Mr. Hislop, together with
Lieutenant Puckle, rode over to Tákulghát along with Mr. Jackson, an
assistant overseer, and some workmen, to excavate those Druidical
remains. I was busy that morning at Bori, and did not join them at
Tákulghát till eleven o'clock. Captain Mackenzie did not go till
eleven o'clock. Lieutenant Puckle returned to Borí, leaving Mr·
Hislop and myself at Tákulghát.

Just then we (that is, Mr. Hislop and myself) took breakfast in a
tent, close to the place where Mr. Jackson and his workmen were dig-
ging. Immediately after breakfast Mr. Hislop read the 5th Chapter
of first Thessalonians. On referring to that chapter you may perhaps
regard it as a providential coincidence that a man should read out that
particular chapter on the morning of the day, in the evening of
which he was unexpectedly to die. But I believe my recollection is
clear that this was the chapter. It is specially preparatory for the
cutting off of life in the midst of health and strength. He then offered
up a prayer as usual. I remember that he concluded by soliciting the
divine blessing on all that had been, and was still being done for the
spiritual conversion of the heathen in this land. After that he observed at some length on the efficiency of the Divine word in convincing
the human conscience. He said these things with a solemnity and
earnestness that come quite clearly to my remembrance.

After that we walked out and looked at the excavations that had
been made, and the various articles of iron and pottery that were being
exhumed. He remarked on the external appearance of the country,
which was that morning fresh and green, the sky being stormy, with
occasional sunshine. He said that this visit recalled to his recollection
a period of fourteen years ago, when he first saw the place, and since
which he had not seen it. He alluded to a former colleague, Mr.
Hunter, in whose company, I think, he said that he had first visited
Tákulghát.

Alluding to ordinary and public affairs, he remarked, that men whose conduct was conscientious before God were those best to be trusted in all affairs of life.

Then we walked about, looking at the ancient circles of stone, and speculating on the character, habits, and institutions of the people who raised them, or rather who arranged them. He thought that all the remains then before us were tombs and burial-places. I asked him whether he supposed that these people had any temples or such like places of worship. He said he thought not; that probably they worshipped some spirit, or some of the elements; and that perhaps they had sacred groves, but nothing more. He observed that every one of the circles of stones had one outside stone towards the east. I asked him whether he thought that these people were migratory in their habits. He did not give a positive opinion on that, but said that the large number of circles, or supposed tombs, indicated that a considerable population must have resided at this spot for some time; that there were, he believed, some eighty of these circles, in each of which at least one person or perhaps several persons had been interred. He added that it was not possible to tell how many persons had been buried, inasmuch as the bodies had been burned, and the others only interred. He said that when the Hindus first came to this part of India, they probably found these people in possession, and conquered them; that then, he supposed, they became mingled with the lower castes of Hindus; that the dwellings of the conquered were swept off the ground; and that these curious burialplaces were all that remained. We then went to the top of a hillock close by, and pointed out the various rows and cross rows of these stone circles extending over the plain.

Descending from this hillock, we met some natives from the village, among whom was a man who had, some fifteen years before, assisted Mr. Hislop in examining the circles in this very place. They recognised each other, and conversed about those times. Then we met a Maráthá gentleman of high rank (Núnájiráo), who owned a large village in the neighbourhood. Mr. Hislop asked what had been done regarding the school in that village; and by his advice I gave Núnájiráo various particular directions regarding the enlargement and improvement of this school, and the Náná went off to execute them. At that time Mr. Hislop said that he would, if possible, visit that school, and also another Government school on his way back to Nágpur the next day.

We then repaired to the tent and sat down. Mr. Hislop began mentioning various forms of infidelity which he had known at different times to exist in sections of Anglo-Indian society; adding, however, that there was much less now-a-days. He then adverted to the fear that an actual infidel must probably entertain of death. He thought that a hardened infidel must have an apprehension (though perhaps unacknowledged) of future punishment, and that even the thought of absolute annihilation after this life, if really entertained, must be awful. We then began speculating as to whether any person could possibly persuade himself of annihilation after physical death.

Mr. Hislop then asked me if I had read Guthrie's Sermons, and alluded to the vigorous nautical imagery contained therein; remarking that the waters of the sea afforded many awful physical illustrations of those spiritual dangers against which the preacher had to warn men. He then alluded to recent discussions at home regarding the Apocrypha, remarking that it ought never to be placed on a level with the Scriptures, and that if it were read authoritatively, or bound up in the same volume with the Bible, there was danger of its being taken as a part of the inspired word of God. He affirmed the perfect inspiration of Scripture, and the extreme danger of private judgment being permitted to consider which parts of Scripture were to be believed absolutely, and which not. Thence he turned to the Free Church of Scotland, to the purity of its origin, and to the disinterestedness of its founders. He added that its leaders were men who had suffered for their principles, and were men of great power and might.

The above was the last serious conversation which he ever held. It was now afternoon. I proposed that we should go back to Borí. He said that I had better start, as there might be business awaiting me; that he would stay a little, and classify the various things that had been exhumed from the circles, and would examine the school at Túkulghát, and would be in time for dinner at Borí.

I then looked at the various things which were being classified and started for Borí, seeing Mr. Hislop no more. That evening, about 8 o'clock, a horse of mine, on which Mr. Hislop was to ride home from Túkulghát, cantered up riderless to the bungalow at Borí, where Lieutenant Puckle and I then were. This led us to apprehend that Mr. Hislop had been detained and lost his horse, or possibly had met with some accident. I instantly despatched two parties in search of him with torches, it being then dark. One of their party was accompanied by the torch-bearer who had just accompanied me on the same road, and the other by the horsekeeper of the horse I had just ridden. These parties searched the ground in different directions, between Borí and Tákulghát; and not finding him, came on to Tákulghát. Midway they found a small stream with water in it, fordable at some places, but at others deep and rapid. At Tákulghát they enquired of Mr. Jackson regarding the object of their search. Mr. Jackson said that Mr. Hislop had left Tákulghát for Borí about dusk that evening, and that as he had not arrived at Borí, and had not been met with midway by the searching parties, something must have happened. Mr. Jackson then went, together with the two searching parties, and fresh torches to the stream already mentioned. They went to a part of it where the water, when the parties last saw it, had been deep and rapid. In the meanwhile, even in that short interval, the water had rapidly subsided; and there they found Mr. Hislop in the bed of the stream, drowned. The body was at once brought to Borí, and examined by a medical officer. Every effort at resuscitation was made without avail. The water had rapidly risen to a height of some ten feet above the bed, and had as rapidly fallen. When the searching party first arrived, the body must have been deep below the muddy turbid waters, and was not visible; when they returned shortly afterwards, the water had subsided from a depth of ten feet, to a depth of three feet, and then the body was found. The accident must have happened about half-past seven, or a quarter to eight, and the body was found soon after ten o'clock. The arrival of the horse at Borí occurred a few minutes after eight, so that Mr. Hislop must have passed beyond human aid, even before we had the first notice of danger.

It appears that he was alone when this melancholy occurrence took place, and therefore the exact manner of its occurrences can be inferred only. But from enquiry made that very night, it is ascertained that about evening he proceeded from the tent to the village of Tákulghát close by, having arranged the several articles of antiquarian interest which had been discovered. This was about sunset. Mr. Jackson was the last European that saw him alive. In the village he examined the school in the presence of the villagers. This was the last act he there performed. He then mounted the horse, and rode off for Borí. It must have been getting dark. He might have taken a guide or a torch-bearer, as such were already in the village. There were two mounted orderlies of mine there; but he doubtless thought the road perfectly safe, being through cultivated ground, when he had passed over once that day, and twice the day before. And indeed the road was perfectly safe, ordinarily. But on that particular evening, a stream which runs past Tákulghát had become suddenly swollen by rain, which had fallen in the neighbouring hills. Into this larger stream there falls the lesser stream intervening between Borí and Tákulghát. And it appears that when the larger stream becomes suddenly flushed with the flood, it throws a back-water into the lesser stream. It was this back-water which filled the little stream as above described. The stream itself is narrow; not more than five or six yards broad, but its bed is more than ten feet deep. It is ordinarily empty; and was so empty when Mr. Hislop had previously seen it. But its depth was very variable : and at places it was fordable even when filled with water. I had myself that evening forded it with entire safety. I had also told a servant to wait at or near the stream, and to show Mr. Hislop the best place to cross at. This man was looking out for Mr. Hislop, but did not meet him.

Mr. Hislop, then, left Tákulghát about dusk on horseback. For a short time after leaving the village the horsekeeper was with him. But coming to open, smooth ground, Mr. Hislop cantered on, leaving the horsekeeper behind. This man returned then to Tákulghát, intending to come on to Borí in company with other servants; he was the last person who saw Mr. Hislop alive. Mr. Hislop must then have cantered on for half a mile and more, till he came to this little stream, which is a mile distant from Tákulghát, and two miles from Borí. Arriving at the stream, he must have ridden into it, supposing the water to be shallow. The fact of water being there may perhaps have struck him as peculiar, but he knew that it was generally empty, and doubtless supposed that it did not contain much water now. Moreover, it was getting dark. In reality, however, at that particular point the water was deep, and the horse on getting into it may have plunged. Certainly I infer from examination of the bridle and saddle, that both rider and horse must have been immersed ; and that the rider was violently disengaged from the animal. He clung for a moment to the grassy bank and then sunk. The horse was a strong, quiet, and steady animal; he recovered himself and got across the stream without the lamented rider. Life must have been extinct within a few minutes after submergence.

And thus befel an accident which, though to human apprehension most melancholy, is yet to spiritual apprehension a cause of thankfulness to the divine will. For we know by faith that the deceased is removed to the presence of God, while we are left to labour on amidst all the doubts and uncertainties of the world. It is a precept that we should live each day as if it might be our last. Now, it is a fact that

Mr. Hislop's last conversation on earth was of a deeply serious import, and that his last act was one of enlightened kindness to ignorant natives.

Though we may not be sorry as those without hope, yet we may humbly acknowledge the judgments of Providence, which are often most strikingly manifested by the sudden removal from amongst us of the best and wisest, in the very zenith of their usefulness. The merits of Mr. Hislop's missionary labours are well known, and will be long remembered. The zeal of his spiritual ministrations among his own countrymen is thankfully regarded by many. He did, moreover, accomplish much by way of maintaining a high moral and intellectual standard among all classes at Nágpur, European and Native. During many years his educational efforts diffused among the natives the influences of Christianity. Even now, natives of intelligence are saying that the loss of his benevolence and knowledge will be severely felt. He was further gifted with scientific ability and aptitude calculated to afford important aid in material improvement; in the good government of the natives, and in the advancement of practical knowledge. He had, in short, by personal character and excellence become a real and living institution at Nágpur. His death is regarded not only as a private, but also a public misfortune.

That you and your children may receive from above that consolation which can alone mitigate such a bereavement, is the hope of the large circle of friends who cherish your late husband's memory with the highest respect and regard.

Believe me to be yours sincerely,

R. TEMPLE.

WORKS BY DR. WILSON.

Procurable only in India.

EXPOSURE OF THE HINDU RELIGION, in Reply to Mor Bhatta Dándekar, in Marathi. Price One Rupee.

SECOND EXPOSURE OF THE HINDU RELIGION, in Reply to Náráyan Ráo of Sátárá, including Strictures on the Vedánta. Price One Rupee.

THE RUDIMENTS OF HEBREW GRAMMAR, in Maráthí. Price Two Rupees.

REFUTATION OF MUHAMMADISM, in Reply to Hájí Muhammad Háshim, in Hindustání. Third Edition. Price Eight Annas, stitched; to Natives, Two Annas.

REFUTATION OF MUHAMMADISM, in Persian. Price Eight Annas, stitched; to Natives, Two Annas.

ELEMENTARY CATECHISM, separately in English, Maráthí, and Gujarátí. Tenth Edition. Price One Anna.

LETTER TO THE JAINA PRIESTS OF PALITANA, in Gujarátí. Second Edition.

THE NATURE OF GOD AND THE CHARACTER OF TRUE WORSHIPPERS, in Maráthí. Eighth Edition.

IDIOMATICAL EXERCISES, illustrative of the Phraseology and Structure of the English and Maráthí Languages. Fourth Edition. Price Two Rupees, Four Annas.

THE WAY OF SALVATION, in Hindustání.

THE PURITY AND INTEGRITY OF THE SCRIPTURES, in Hindustání.

PRAYER FOR RAIN, in Maráthí.

THE SIX SCHOOLS OF PHILOSOPHY: An outline of a Lecture delivered at the request of the Bombay Dialectic Association, 18th March, 1856. Price Eight Annas.

JUSTIFICATION BY FAITH ALONE : a Discourse.

Preparing for publication.

TWO EXPOSURES OF THE HINDU RELIGION, in Reply to Brahmanical Controversialists; including a General View of the Sacred Literature and Mythology of the Hindus. Second Edition.

IN THE PRESS, AND SPEEDILY WILL BE PUBLISHED:

INDIAN CASTE: What it Is, What it Does, and What should be Done with it. By JOHN WILSON, D.D., F.R.S.